KANYE WEST QUOTES

Dear Nora,

I hope this book will inspire you to work even harder on improving and beautifying your inner Kanye

love, Natalia

21.05.2018

Kanye West Quotes

Author: Sreechinth C

DEDICATION

This book, 'Kanye West Quotes' is dedicated at the feet of Almighty.

"If you have the opportunity to play this game of life you need to appreciate every moment, a lot of people don't appreciate the moment until it's passed."

- Kanye West

DISCLAIMER

This book contains quotes and sayings of Kanye West. Those are included here considering them as quotations which he expressed. The author does not owe any copyright or responsibility over the wordings.

Although the author and publisher have made every effort to ensure that the information in this book was correct at press time, the author and publisher do not assume and hereby disclaim any liability to any party for any loss, damage, or disruption caused by errors or omissions, whether such errors or omissions result from negligence, accident, or any other cause.

Table of Contents

ACKNOWLEDGMENTS   1

ABOUT KANYE WEST   3

QUOTES OF KANYE WEST   6

EXTRAS   73

     Author's Request 73

     Related Books 74

     Best Works of the Publication........................81

ACKNOWLEDGMENTS

Sincerely showing thankfulness to all those who participated and supported directly and indirectly in the release of this book.

ABOUT KANYE WEST

The most acclaimed American musicians of 21st century, Kanye West is also well known as record producer and fashion designer. As one of the most sold artists of all time, he has the maximum number of Grammy Awards with debuting only in this century.

On June 8, 1977, Kanye Omari West's birth was in Atlanta, Georgia. As his parents divorced when he was just three, his childhood got parted in father and mother's homes. At an early age, he showed interest in arts as Kanye wrote poems when he was just five. After graduating from Polaris High School, he joined Chicago University to study painting. But soon realizing it was not his field, he dropped out from college to pursue his musical dreams. The contemporary hip hop culture had much influence on him, yet he start of his musical career as song producer primarily working for the local artists. His breakthrough was the release of Jay Z's album The Blue Print. The later years saw his critical acclaim as the in-house producer of Roc-A-Fella Records. Though he continued the production, his ultimate aim was to become a rapper and tried to test

3

his luck in that which failed utterly as couldn't sign any contracts.

2002 October was his crucial time for him both personally and professionally. He had a fatal accident while he was deriving home from the recording studio leaving fractured jaw. Nevertheless it was a life demanding accident, he used it to change his musical career. With that wired shut jaw, he returned to the studio releasing his debutant album 'The College Dropout'. This was an immense hit selling more than 2 million copies world wide. It banged the 10 prestigious Grammy Awards including the one for the Best Rap Album. 'Late Registration' in 2005 and 'Graduation' in 2007 and 'South side' a collaboration with Commons too made him again the winner of these Awards. Though his career had a shoot up in the following years, he had a much personal in the form of the death of his mother, Donda West. His fourth album '808s & Heartbreak', was In this context and the audience saw a different Kanye with a much slower tempo and a totally different style.

The outspoken and the controversial star was in headlines the next year, 2009, for his stormy behavior on the stage of MTV's Best music video awards. He was against the winner Taylor Swift and wanted Beyonce's Single Ladies as the best. This incident aroused much criticisms, finally prompting him to cut down his musical tour. But the release of his fifth album 'My Beautiful Dark Twisted Fantasy' was just enough to end all the controversies and his name was placed in the top charts. In 2013 with 'Yeezus' and 'Only One' in 2014 Kanye again blow the charts.

Along with the musical career, he is also a fashion icon. He had collaborations with prominent brands Nike, Adidas, Louis Vuitton and Yeezy. He is married to the TV celebrity Kim Kardashian and have two children. In 2016, he released his seventh album, 'Life of Pablo'. Being one of the most awarded artists of all time, Kanye West is the holder of 21 Grammy Awards. Let's explore the words of this most successful musician of the 21st century.

QUOTES OF KANYE WEST

"Come on now! How could you be me and want to be someone else?"

"Okay, everyone please be completely quiet, because I can literally hear a whisper, and it'll throw off my stream of consciousness, and when I get my stream of consciousness going that's when I give the best, illest quotes. Literally, a whisper can throw it off."

"If I don't win, the award show loses credibility."

"We've been sold a concept of joy through advertising. It was somehow sold to us through a Gucci bag or something."

"They say your attitude determines your latitude..."

"I'm a creative genius and there's no other way to word it."

"Keep rocking', and keep knocking' Whether you Louis Vuitton it up or Reebok in' You see the hate, that they're serving' on a platter So what we gone' have, dessert or disaster?"

"I know I got to be right now Cause I can't get much wronger"

"You have the power to let power go"

"I used to have the Virgin music stores, and I would go there and just go up the escalator and say to myself, 'I'm soaking in these last moments of anonymity.' I knew I was going to make it this far; I knew that this was going to happen"

"George Bush doesn't care about black people... They're saying black families are looting and white families are just looking for food... they're giving the Army permission to shoot us."

"I can analyze people's intentions. Immediately. That's just a warning. To everyone."

"I'm the rap version of Dave Chappelle. I'm not saying' I'm nearly as talented as Chappelle when it comes to political and social commentary, but like him, I'm laughing to keep from crying."

"They say, he must had an angel, cuss look how death missed his ass. Unbreakable, what you thought they'd call me Mr. Glass?"

"You want to be upper class, you want to be first class, but when the plane crash, everybody dead,"

"Society has put up so many boundaries, so many limitations on what's right and wrong that it's almost impossible to get a pure thought out. It's like a little kid, a little boy, looking at colors, and no one told him what colors are good, before somebody tells you shouldn't like pink because that's for girls, or you'd instantly become a gay two-year-old. Why would anyone pick blue over pink? Pink is obviously a better color. Everyone's born confident, and everything's taken away from you"

"I see stuff from the future, and I'm such a futurist that I have to slow down and talk in the present."

"My goal, if I was going to do art, fine art, would have been to become Picasso or greater. That always sounds so funny to people, comparing yourself to someone in the past that has done so much, and in your life you're not even allowed to think that you can do as much. That's a mentality that suppresses humanity."

"I want to build the biggest apparel company in human history."

"I'm not a corny-ass booty freak! I'm the greatest musician of all-time."

"I've had meetings where a guy actually told me, "What we're trying to figure out is how we can control you." In the meeting, to me! Why do you want to control me?"

"Taking 1,000 meetings attempting to get backing to do clothing..."

"I think I'm a whole lot to handle. I definitely am, on every aspect. I'm the video director. I'm the graphics designer. I'm the rapper. I'm the visionary. I'm the music producer. I'm the executive producer. I'm just going to end it off to be poetic: I'm the future of music."

"We going to touch the sky"

"When I was in fourth grade I was drawing Jordans when my mama couldn't afford them."

"This album is moments that I haven't done before, like just my voice and drums. What people call a rant - but put it next to just a drumbeat, and it cuts to the level of, like, Run-D.M.C. or KRS-One."

"There's nothing I really wanted to do in life that I wasn't able to get good at. That's my skill. I'm not really specifically talented at anything except for the ability to learn. That's what I do. That's what I'm here for."

"I spent two of my checks in telemarketing when I was 18-years-old on my first pair of Gucci slippers. This was before H&M and Zara, you couldn't just find cool stuff when you were growing up. And to me, I care a lot about cool stuff. It means something to me."

"Every interview I'm representing you making you proud. Reach for the stars so if you fall you land on a cloud."

"The dinosaurs aren't remembered for much more than their bones. When humanity's gone, what do we give to this little planet that we're on, and what could we do collectively, removing the pride?"

"You know that one auntie, you don't want to be rude, ...But every holiday, nobody eating' her food."

"Don't say you don't know! It's because of Kim. Meaning there's no photo that I would have put up by myself, or next to one of my smarty friends, that would have got that amount of likes. So now you take this photo that has that amount of likes, and it has a flower wall from the same guy who does the Lanvin shows, and it has a couture Givenchy dress and Givenchy tuxedo in it. That's the point. Now the thing that is the most popular is also communicating the highest level of creativity. The concept of Kimye has more cultural significance than what Page Six could write."

"It was a strike against me that I didn't wear baggy jeans and jerseys and that I never hustled, never sold drugs."

"This dark diction has become America's addiction."

"You've got to be really dialed into exactly who you are to the one hundredth power or you're just everyone else."

"I don't particularly like photos of myself, though."

"Being fresh is more important than having money."

"People want fame and I would never tell a person to not want that, because it's fucking awesome. Actually."

"Why would anyone pick blue over pink? Pink is obviously a better color."

"Kris Jenner and the family, they have the power of communication. This is the number one communications company."

"All this role model bullshit; you don't have any extra responsibilities because you made some good songs! Your only responsibility is to make good songs."

"I was always considered this crazy hothead kid, but I would always just go and just really break bread with someone who I respected. I will completely bow to anybody I respect."

"I remember when both Gnarls Barkley and Justin Timberlake lost for Album of the Year at the Grammys, and I looked at Justin, and I was like: 'Do you want me to go onstage for you? You know, do you want me to fight?"

"Why, if someone is good in one field can they not be accepted or given the slightest opportunity to express and be creative in other fields?"

"I am Warhol. I am the No. 1 most impactful artist of our generation. I am Shakespeare in the flesh."

"I would rather sit in a factory than sit in a Maybach."

"I'm going to say this tonight because 20 years from now, 30 years from now, 40 years from now, I might not be able to say it, but I can say it tonight... You are now watching the greatest living rock star on the planet"

"So few hip-hop artists have ever advanced. Their songs on their seventh, eighth albums sound exactly like the songs on their first album. More than an artist, I'm a real person- and real people grow. And I want to just sing my growth."

"People asked me to change my name for 808s...I think the fact that I can't sing that well is what makes "808s" so special."

"I get to represent somebody I don't think is getting represented right now. The regular dude: the guy who believes in God but still likes pussy."

"I don't know what's better: getting laid or getting paid. I just know when I'm getting one, the other's getting away."

"You can't look at a glass half full or empty if it's overflowing."

"I looked at Justin, and I was like: 'Do you want me to go onstage for you?'"

"As kids we used to laugh/Who knew that life would move this fast? Who knew I'd have to look at you through a glass? And look, tell me you aren't did it, you aren't did it And if you did, then that's family business."

"I think about things to put them in a place where I don't have to think about them anymore. Say if I had a child with a really bad mom, I would have to think more than if I had a child with a good mom. I'm just doing my homework early."

"Kim Kardashian is just a funny person in general."

"I don't like walking around with people thinking I'm doing uncool s--, because there's nothing I'm doing that's uncool. It's all innovative. You just might not understand it yet. But it's cool. Family is super cool. Going home to one girl every night is super cool. Just going home and getting on the floor and playing with your child is super cool. Not wearing a red leather jacket, and just looking like a dad and s--, is like super cool. Having someone that I can call Mom again. That s-- is super cool."

"Benjamin Franklin didn't win 21 Grammys right?"

"I'm my favorite rapper."

"Got a light skinned friend, look like Michael Jackson, Got a dark skinned friend, look like Michael Jackson."

"I could still do a suit, I just wouldn't have done that exact lapel situation."

"I don't like facts, because facts get in the way of my feelings."

"This one Corbusier lamp was like, my greatest inspiration ... I'm a minimalist in a rapper's body."

"People say, 'What do you mean you want to help the world, but you're so concerned about fashion?' It's illegal to be naked. It is something that is extremely important."

"So I can go and let out everything that I feel about every bogus weekly cover, every single bogus skit, every single rumor and barber shop-everything that people feel is ok to treat celebrities like zoo animals, or act like what they're saying is not serious, or their lives are not serious or their dreams are not serious."

"Slavery is more mental than anything"

"Couldn't afford a car so he named his daughter Alexis"

"You telling' me people don't look at Kanye West like the Glitch."

"My music is rock. I listen to Red Hot Chili Peppers and I listen to one of my songs, and if I don't give you the same emotion, then I go back and re-spit."

"Beauty has been stolen from the people and is being sold back to them as luxury."

"Bravery and courage is walking into pain and knowing that something better is on the other side"

"What I'm saying is we're making product with chitlins. T-shirts! That's the most we can make."

"I am a black new wave artist."

"I'm going to be the first hip-hop designer and because of that I'm going to be bigger than Wal-Mart."

"It don't got to be Mother's Day, or your birthday, for me to just call and say Hey Mama"

"50 told me go head and switch the style up and if they hate, let them hate, watch the money pile up."

"I'm a mix of a 14-year-old high schooler and a 60-year-old guy. It can never fall into the 30s or the 40s. It has to be 100 percent 60 or 100 percent 14, no in between."

"People say I've got a bad reputation. I think I've got the best reputation in the building."

"They say your attitude determines your latitude ..."

"I felt like I was definitely robbed, and I refuse to give any politically correct bullshit ass comment. I was the best new artist this year."

"I'm a let you finish, but the French Revolution had the best severed heads of all time."

"Well, I just don't want to talk to America about my family. Like, this is my baby. This isn't America's baby."

"Racism is still alive they just be concealing it"

"I feel like I'm too busy writing history to read it."

"It is true you can be successful without [college], but this is a hard world, a real world, and you want every advantage you can have. I would suggest to people to do all that you can. When I dropped out of school, I had worked in the music industry and had checks cut in my name from record labels and had a record deal on the table, and when I wasn't successful and Columbia said, 'We'll call you,' I had to go back and work a telemarketing job, go back to the real world, and that's how life is. Life is hard. Take advantage of your opportunities."

"I am in the lineage of Gil Scott-Heron, great activist-type artists. But I'm also in the lineage of a Miles Davis - you know, that liked nice things also."

"It's crazy that we live in a world where if your super positive and super creative...it's scary. Because what does that tell you about the mentality of most people if your scared of like...positivity."

"I'm a blowfish. I'm not a shark, I'm a blowfish. So that perfect example about me hitting my head [he walked into a street sign and it was caught by paparazzi], it's like a blowfish. I wasn't coming out of my house going to a paparazzi's house to attack them. I'm defending my family in front of my own house. I'm defending my name as someone's screaming something negative at me. That's a blowfish. People have me pinned as a shark or a predator in some way, and in no way am I that. I wouldn't want to hurt anyone. I want to defend people. I want to help people."

"Creative output, you know, is just pain. I'm going to be cliché for a minute and say that great art comes from pain."

"I feel like now I have an amazing wife, a super smart child and the opportunity to create in two major fields. Before I had those outlets, my ego was all I had."

"Living well eliminates the need for revenge."

"I will be the leader of a company that ends up being worth billions of dollars, because I got the answers."

"Okay, for me, first of all, dopeness is what I like the most."

"I go all the way back to the Hot Boys days and being 13, listening to this dude. Just remembering the staple he put on the game back then all the way to now, to have that longevity years beyond it. So for him to actually acknowledge what I'm doing right now and seeing it as a path, the same way the longevity he created, it's a great feeling to actually share that same stage and a moment with him. Wayne isn't no new jack to this game. He influenced a lot of styles and a lot of sounds. I would say I was influenced by a recent sound and flow, and cadence that he brung to the game."

""Dark Fantasy" was my long, backhanded apology. You know how people give a backhanded compliment? It was a backhanded apology. It was like, all these raps, all these sonic acrobatics. I was like: "

"Let me show you guys what I can do, and please accept me back. You want to have me on your shelves.""

"What if you're Gaudi and you know you're the best architect and everyone is saying that you're saying you're the best architect the wrong way?"

"Everyone's born confident, and everything's taken away from you."

"I understand culture. I am the nucleus."

"I want to shout out the stars on the walk of fame because they said something about they're not going to put my girl on the Walk of Fame because she's a reality star. It's like, people are so dated and not modern. There's no way that Kim Kardashian should not have a star on the Walk of Fame. It's ridiculous concepts. I'm just going to give y'all the truth and you're just going to love it."

"I always feel like I can do anything. That's the main thing people are controlled by: thoughts and perceptions of yourself... If you're taught you can't do anything, you won't do anything"

"I wouldn't even say that I'm a rapper. I'd say I'm more of a messenger."

"Brands are selling our self-esteem back to us, through association. We need to own our brands."

"You want me to be great, but you don't ever want me to say I'm great?"

"I believe that everyone is a fashion insider, because it's illegal to be naked."

"I don't even listen to rap. My apartment is too nice to listen to rap in."

"I wake up every day trying to give something back to you that you can rock to and be proud of."

"Respect my trendsetting abilities. Once that happens, everyone wins."

"Nothing is promised in life except death."

"Recognize and embrace your flaws so you can learn from them. Sometimes it takes a little polishing to truly shine."

"If you're a Kanye West fan, you're not a fan of me, you're a fan of yourself. You will believe in yourself. I'm just the espresso."

"Great art comes from great artists. There's a bunch of people that are hurt that still couldn't have made the album that was super-polarizing and redefined the sound of radio."

"My goal, if I was going to do art, fine art, would have been to become Picasso or greater."

"That that don't kill me, can only make me stronger."

"I think what Kanye West is going to mean is something similar to what Steve Jobs means."

"I didn't want to play it boring and safe. I also didn't want to innovate too much. Second albums, man, they're even scarier than first ones."

"I'm a pop enigma. I live and breathe every element in life. I rock a bespoke suit and I go to Harold's for fried chicken. It's all these things at once, because, as a taste maker, I find the best of everything. There's certain things that black people are the best at and certain things that white people are the best at. Whatever we as black people are the best at, I'm go get that. Like, on Christmas I don't want any food that tastes white. And when I go to purchase a house, I don't want my credit to look black."

"Every time I crash the Internet, it's like this little drop of truth. Every time I say something that's extremely truthful out loud, it literally breaks the Internet. So what are we getting all of the rest of the time?"

"I will die for the art & what I believe in. The art isn't always going to be polite."

"I won't go into a big spiel about reincarnation, but the first time I was in the Gucci store in Chicago was the closest I've ever felt to home."

"Would you believe in what you believe in if you were the only one who believed it?"

"And I can't even go to the grocery store without some ones that's clean and a shirt with a team/It seems we living the American dream but people highest up got the lowest self esteem/The prettiest people do the ugliest things for the road to riches and diamond rings."

"Sometimes I feel the music is the only medicine."

"Drug dealer buy Jordans, crackhead buy crack. And a white man get paid off of all of that."

"As we live, our hearts turn colder. Cause pain is what we go through, as we become older. We get insulted by others, lose trust for those others. We get back stabbed by friends. It becomes harder for us to give others a hand. We get our heart broken by people we love, even that we give them all we have. Then we lose family over time. What else could rust the heart more over time? Black gold."

"Hate and love are very similar emotions. The opposite of love is you don't care."

"The idea of Kanye and vanity are like, synonymous."

"If it wasn't for race mixing, there'd be no video girls."

"But I think I'm on track to do something even bigger. I liberate minds with my music. That's more important than liberating a few people from apartheid or whatever."

"When you're the absolute best, you get hated on the most."

"And wouldn't change by the change, or the game, or the fame, when he came, in the game, he made his own name"

"Love is infectious. You know, God is infectious-God flowing through us and us being little-baby creators and s--. But His energy and His love and what He wants us to have as people and the way He wants us to love each other, that is infectious. Like they said in Step Brothers: Never lose your dinosaur. This is the ultimate example of a person never losing his dinosaur. Meaning that even as I grew in cultural awareness and respect and was put higher in the class system in some way for being this musician, I never lost my dinosaur."

"Death is promised. So what do you do with your life? How do you make the most of it? How do you make your voice the loudest?"

"People let their frustrations out on me. I love Kanye West. They say the opposite of that. But I'm not going to say that. I'm only going to say what I'm want to put into the universe."

"I was never really good at anything except for the ability to learn."

"You know, if Michael Jordan can scream at the refs, me as Kanye West, as the Michael Jordan of music, can go and say, 'This is wrong.'"

"If I was just a fan of music, I would think that I was the number one artist in the world."

"Never do coke with an intern … they may not be 21"

"I will go down as the voice of this generation, of this decade, I will be the loudest voice."

"Take your diamonds and throw them up like you're bulimic. Yeah, the beat cold, but the flow is anemic."

"Let the music defuse all the tension."

"I can always tell if a band has a British rhythm section due to the gritty production."

"It's like this, by not giving my album a classic rating, you diminish your magazine's credibility. And that's real."

"I think that people don't make the most of their lives. So, you know, for me, it seems like it's the beginning of me rattling the cage, of making some people nervous. And people are strategically trying to do things to mute my voice in some way or make me look like I'm a lunatic or pinpoint the inaccuracies in my grammar to somehow take away from the overall message of what I'm saying."

"I've known my mom since I was zero years old. She is quite dope."

"I will spark a generation of thinkers who will question traditional thought until they find the absolute truth"

"If I was more complacent and I let things slide, my life would be easier, but you all wouldn't be as entertained. My misery is your pleasure."

"People always try to box you in to what they know you best for."

"If you fall on concrete, that's your ass fault"

"Love your haters - they're your biggest fans"

"Fusion is the future. The mixing of ideas. The two lunch tables working together. Humanity...we're 1 people."

"I am not a fan of books."

"Fur pillows are hard to actually sleep on."

"For me giving up is way harder than trying."

"I'm always fighting either to have a house work with us or to head a house. It's a lifestyle I can totally see: the future, modern Versailles, modern Versace, modern Calabasas, paparazzi, celebrity language. I just want to build a collection that's around me and my wife and my kids."

"Just know that if you want to be a boxer you're going to get your face beaten constantly but then you may end up being a Mayweather or an Ali at the end of the day."

"I feel that I'm very blessed. But with great blessings come great responsibility."

"I woke up early this morning' with a new state of mind/ A creative way to rhyme without using' knives and guns"

"If you don't make Christmas presents, meaning making something that's so emotionally connected to people, don't talk to me."

"I'm going to sit here on this runway until I'm at the end of it. Because that's that thing that people slave over. That's that thing that people are slaves to. That's that thing that I'm a slave to."

"I just close my eyes and act like I'm a 3-year-old. I try to get as close to a childlike level as possible because we were all artists back then. So you just close your eyes and think back to when you were as young as you can remember and had the least barriers to your creativity."

"So I hope that there are people out there laughing. Laugh loud, please. Laugh until your lungs give out because I will have the last laugh."

"The plan was to drink until the pain is over, But what's worse, the pain or the hangover?"

"If you have the opportunity to play this game of life you need to appreciate every moment. a lot of people don't appreciate the moment until it's passed."

"Nobody's going to be bigger than Eminem."

"No one man should have all that power."

"Like, this is my baby. This isn't America's baby."

"It's a tough world out there. You're going to prepare yourself for politics, bad bosses, hating employees - and usually when you're the absolute best, you get hated on the most."

"In the night, I hear them talk. Coldest story ever told. Somewhere far along this road he lost his soul."

"Nike told me, 'We can't give you royalties because you're not a professional athlete.' I told them 'I'll go to the Garden and play one-on-no-one.' I'm a performance athlete!"

"If you see a black family, it's looting, but if it's a white family they are looking for food."

"I'm Kan, the Louis Vouitton don. Bought my mom purse, now she Louis Vuitton mom. I didn't play the hand I was dealt I changed my card. I prayed to the skies and I changed my stars. I went to the malls and I balled too hard. Oh My God is that a Black card. I turned around and replied why yes, but I prefer the term African American Express"

"Don't Ever fix your lips like collagen And say something when you going end up apologizing"

"You have to be able to swim in backlash."

"We buy our way out of jail but we can't buy freedom, We buy a lot of clothes when we don't really need them, Things we buy to cover up what's inside."

"An artist's career doesn't happen in the cycle of one week of news. An artist's career happens in a lifetime, and if you're a true artist you're willing to die for what you believe in."

"Everything I'm not makes me everything I am"

"The media crucify me like they did Christ."

"Here's something that's contrary to popular belief: I actually don't like thinking. I think people think I like to think a lot. And I don't. I do not like to think at all."

"If you talking 'bout classics, do my name get brought up?"

"People say to me 'you're successful, what are you crying about?'. I'm crying about the people. I'm crying about their daughters. Our daughters, as one family. What good is it. What good is anything that everyone can't have. Every ism. They think we're done with racism. What about elitism, what about separatism, what about classism? That's all."

"One of my biggest Achilles' heels has been my ego. And if I, Kanye West, the very person, can remove my ego, I think there's hope for everyone."

"I'm giving all that I have in this life. I'm opening up my notebook and I'm saying everything in there out loud."

"Whenever y'all are in the store from and y'all are trying to decide whether or not to get something, think if you saw me wear it before or not, and if I have, then it's okay."

"I'm on the pursuit of awesomeness, excellence is the bare minimum."

"What happens if a drone falls right next to her?"

"George Bush doesn't care about black people."

"I'm really happy I'm me because if I wasn't I'd be scared. If you want that Number One spot you need to listen to my album and try to beat it."

"I refuse to follow the rules where society tries to control people with low self esteem."

"Because when you keep on diminishing art and not respecting the craft and smacking people in their face after they deliver monumental feats of music, you're disrespectful to inspiration, and we as musicians have to inspire people who go to work every day, and they listen to that Beyonce album and they feel like it takes them to another place."

"There are people who have figured out the exact, you know, Kanye West formula, the mix between "Graduation" and "808s," and were able to become more successful at it."

"Believe in your flyness...conquer your shyness"

"I think my sense of humor is really dark and super twisted and stuff like that. It's like, "Is this a funny joke for real? Or am I just rich?" See? That was funny."

"Me and my girl split the buffet at KFC."

"As a man I am flawed, but my music is perfect."

"I am not here to argue about his facial features. Or here to convert atheists into believers. I'm just trying to say the way school need teachers the way Kathie Lee needed Regis that's the way you will need Jesus."

"I don't understand why they tripping, If you ask me, Flow is just as nice as, I admit the propane, I just spit, probably, Just raise the gas prices, Everybody in the club, Try and get as fresh as me, What you want dog, Trying to stay recession free, And spit, refreshingly,"

"I worked a telemarketing job. I always worked those because I always knew how to talk to people and I always knew how to sell because my father was a salesman. He used to sell vacuum cleaners, payroll services to companies, so that was natural for me to go into sales."

"The dinosaurs are remember only by their bones. What will we be remembered for with humanity?"

"I use too much of my brain and need to let some of it rest."

"I guess every superhero need his theme music."

"Memories have to be our most painful blessing."

"For the person that wrote that, were they involved with anything last year that was as culturally significant as the Yeezus tour or that album? ... The bar was terrible, and the wedding planner didn't approve it with me. I was having issues with this wedding planner the entire time on approvals, and I get there and they threw some weird plastic bar there."

"I don't expect to be understood at all."

"All I need is the breakthrough. The joint-venture for my clothing. Same as Stella McCartney has…"

"I'm typing so fucking hard I might break my fucking Mac book Air!"

"Life is a bitch depending how you dress her."

"Ralph Lauren was boring before I worn him"

"To be a visionary, all you have to do is make decisions based off of your eyes instead of your ears and your memory."

"She, Kim Kardashian was always my muse, now she's become other designers' muses."

"What I feel like - 'cause I want to be married, of course - I feel like the type of girl I would be with is a fellow superhero. So we get that 'already flying and now we're just flying together' thing."

"But for me to have the opportunity to stand in front of a bunch of executives and present myself, I had to hustle in my own way. I can't tell you how frustrating it was that they didn't get that. No joke - I'd leave meetings crying all the time."

"Wait 'till I get my money right.."

"You basically can say anything to someone on an email or text as long as you put LOL at the end."

"Never stop fighting no matter what anyone says. If it's in your gut, your soul, there's nothing, no worldly possession that should come between you and your expression."

"My music isn't just music- its medicine."

"I feed the branches of the people."

"Rome wasn't built in a day, and the internet is our new Rome"

"I am the number one human being in music. That means any person that's living or breathing is number two."

"Black people can be the most conservative, the most discriminating. Especially among ourselves. It wasn't white people who said all black men have to wear baggy jeans."

"I refuse to accept other people's ideas of happiness for me. As if there's a 'one size fits all' standard for happiness."

"We are the creative with teeth. We know ideas are more important than our personal wellbeing."

"I'll say things that are serious and put them in a joke form so people can enjoy them. We laugh to keep from crying."

"I want to make uniforms for my high school basketball team through brand Yeezy."

"There would have been no Beats deal without the Samsung deal. It showed the number one company the importance of connecting with culture,"

"I'm not comfortable with comfort. I'm only comfortable when I'm in a place where I'm constantly learning and growing."

"Thirty-three-years-old, still creating art. It's rage, it's creativity, it's pain, it's hurt, but it's the opportunity to still have my voice get out there through music."

"I am so credible and so influential and so relevant that I will change things."

"I just think that when my confidence meets other people's insecurity, that equals Kanye's arrogant."

"Versace! Versace! Versace! Versace! Versace! Versace! We love Versace. Versace is the greatest designer of all time!"

"I love the fact that I'm bad at [things]."

"Sometimes when I see a bad performance and people still clap... I wonder if they're clapping because they liked what they saw or because they're happy it's over?"

"We rappers are role models."

"Man... ninjas are kind of cool... I just don't know any personally."

"Though it's thousands of miles away Sierra Leone connect to what we go through today Over here, its a drug trade, we die from drugs Over there, they die from what we buy from drugs"

"Visiting my mind is like visiting the Hermes factory. Sh*t is real. You're not going to find a chink. It's 100,000 per cent Jimi Hendrix."

"Sometimes people write novels and they just be so wordy and so self-absorbed. I am not a fan of books ... I like to get information from doing stuff like actually talking to people and living real life."

"I'm not going to sit inside of a corporation for 20 years. The time is now. The time is now to express yourself. The time is now to believe in yourself."

"I had a dream I could buy my way to heaven, when I awoke, I spent that on a NECKLACE..."

"If you a Kanye West fan, you a fan of yourself."

"I'm still just a kid learning about minimalism, and he's a master of it. It's just really such a blessing, to be able to work with him. I want to say that after working with Rick, it humbled me to realize why I hadn't - even though I produced "Watch the Throne"; even though I produced "Dark Fantasy" - why I hadn't won Album of the Year yet."

"For me to say I wasn't a genius I'd just be lying to you and to myself"

"I would say my determination is way higher than my smartness."

"Oh am I late? No, I already graduated And you can live through anything if Magic made it They say I talk with so much emphasis Ooh they so sensitive"

"I used to have insecurity about my finances, then I announced that I had debt, and now I don't have any insecurities."

"My attitude is tattooed that means it's permanent"

"You're not perfect, but you're not your mistakes."

"Both this song 'Black Skinhead', 'I Am a God' and this song were made after Hedi Slimane didn't let me into his first Saint Laurent show."

"I'm a heaven sent instrument. My rhythmatic regimen navigates melodic notes for your soul and your mental. That's why I'm instrumental, vibrations is what I'm into."

"Sometimes people write novels and they just be so wordy and so self-absorbed."

"50 is Eminem's favorite rapper... I'm my favorite rapper."

"You have to think like a designer. You have to establish the trend four seasons before it becomes popular."

"If your job is inspiration you have to go at it at all costs."

"What is the definition of cool? Michael Jackson made "Heal the World." He could do that because he was golden. He was himself. He didn't have to try to be cool. Think about a lot of your favorite bands or groups. Would they make a song called "Heal the World"? No, because they are too concerned about their leather jackets. Ironically, they are probably wearing leather jackets because of Michael Jackson."

"I got to new strategy it's called no strategy. And I got to way to sell more music its called make better music."

"My parents taught me that AIDS was a man-made disease designed to get rid of the undesirable people."

"I'm putting my life at risk, literally! And if I slipped... You never know. And I think about it. I think about my family and I'm like, wow, this is like being a police officer or something, in war or something."

"The way Kathy Lee needs Regis, that's the way I need Jesus."

"As a rapper, I feel like image is always important but even more so than image, I really love clothes, that's why I don't use stylists. I want to do it myself because I really love it."

"I love the fact that I'm bad at [things], you know what I'm saying? I'm forever the 35-year-old 5-year-old. I'm forever the 5-year-old of something."

"We have the ability to approach our race like ants, or we have the ability to approach our race like crabs."

"I try to get as close to a childlike level as possible because we were all artists back then."

"Yeah, I think that I have like, faltered, you know, as a human. My message isn't perfectly defined. I have, as a human being, fallen to peer pressure."

"Time is the only luxury. It's the only thing you can't get back. If you lose your luggage - I'm not going to say the obvious brand of luggage that I'd normally say because I've got a meeting with them soon - if you lose your expensive luggage at the airport, you can get that back. You can't get the time back."

"I gave him his first TV and he needs to remember that."

"When someone comes up and says something like, 'I am a god,' everybody says 'Who does he think he is?' I just told you who I thought I was. A god. I just told you. That's who I think I am."

"They say you can rap about anything except for Jesus, that means guns, sex, lies, video tapes, but if I talk about God my record won't get played Huh?"

"I don't have one regret."

"If you're taught you can't do anything you won't do anything, I was taught I could do everything"

"If anyone's reading this waiting for some type of full-on, flat apology for anything, they should just stop reading right now."

"I know I got angels watching me from the other side."

"I think there are school teachers who are on the exact same mission as me."

"People ask me a lot about my drive. I think it comes from, like, having a sexual addiction at a really young age. Look at the drive that people have to get sex - to dress like this and get a haircut and be in the club in the freezing cold at 3 A.M., the places they go to pick up a girl. If you can focus the energy into something valuable, put that into work ethic"

"I was wearing like, a Juicy Couture men's polo shirt. We weren't there, like, ready for war"

"In America, they want you to accomplish these great feats, to pull off these David Copperfield-type stunts. You want me to be great, but you don't ever want me to say I'm great?"

"I was on the junior team when I was a freshman, that's how good I was. But I wasn't on my eighth-grade team, because some coach - some Grammy, some reviewer, some fashion person, some blah blah blah - they're all the same as that coach."

"I'm the No. 1 living and breathing rock star. I am Axl Rose; I am Jim Morrison; I am Jimi Hendrix."

"Turn that 62 to 125, 125 to 250, 250 to half a million, am not nothing nobody can do with me."

"Having money isn't everything, not having it is."

"I know you can't control everything, and everything is in God's hands ultimately, but I'm going to fight, go out and perform for everybody, I don't care."

"She said, "'Ye can we get married at the mall?" I said, "Look, you need to crawl 'fore you ball Come and meet me in the bathroom stall And show me why you deserve to have it all""

"They say people in your life are seasons and anything that happens is for a reason."

"I got a long road ahead of me to make people believe i'm not actually a huge douche."

"I want to help change the way young people look at school, and hence, the way they look at their futures."

"Thank God I'm not too cool for a seatbelt."

"I know I've been called the Louis Vuitton Don ... I've been called a lot of names ... Due to what happened, so severely, when the red shoes hit the runway, I was forced to change my name to Martin Louis Vuitton the King, Jr. Address me as such."

"Throw your diamonds in the sky if you feel the vibe"

"My favorite body part of Kim's: heart."

"I think that's a responsibility that I have, to push possibilities, to show people, this is the level that things could be at. So when you get something that has the name Kanye West on it, it's supposed to be pushing the furthest possibilities. I will be the leader of a company that ends up being worth billions of dollars, because I got the answers. I understand culture. I am the nucleus."

"I've reached a point in my life where my Truman Show boat has hit the painting."

"This dope money here is Lil Treys scholarship Cause isn't no to tuition for having no ambition And isn't no loans for sitting your ass at home"

"What's the main thing that makes magic? The fact that no one believes that it's possible."

"Look, I can be married to the most beautiful woman in the world, and I am. I can have the most beautiful little daughter in the world, and I have that. But I'm nothing if I can't be me. If I can't be true to myself, they don't mean anything."

"We headed to hell for heaven sakes, well Imma levitate...make the devil wait."

"Fashion breaks my heart."

"In Paris, you're as far as possible from the land of pleasant smiles."

"I am not crazy, I'm just not satisfied."

"My favorite song is "All Along the Watchtower." The Jimi Hendrix cover."

"I'm like a vessel, and God has chosen me to be the voice and the connector."

"I thought my Jesus Piece was so harmless 'Till I see a picture of a Shorty armless"

"Fur pillows are actually hard to sleep on."

"I think I do myself a disservice by comparing myself to Steve Jobs and Walt Disney and human beings that we've seen before. It should be more like Willy Wonka... and welcome to my chocolate factory."

"I fervently believe that, as someone has said before, "When you change the way you look at things, the things you look at change." I want to help change the way young people look at school, and hence, the way they look at their futures."

"The idea of Kanye and vanity are like, synonymous. But I've put myself in a lot of places where a vain person wouldn't put themselves in. Like what's vanity about wearing a kilt?"

"Why everything that's supposed to be bad Make me feel so good?"

"Now that you're gone, it hit us, super hard on Thanksgiving and Christmas, this can't be right, you heard the track I did called this can't be life"

"Starting now, you're just starting to see a glimmer of what the idea of West will mean. So right now, at this age and with this visibility and with the skill sets that Kim is now giving me, I think I have a good chance of success in building something that has longevity, high integrity, high success rate, and is very fulfilling, not only for me creatively but also in adding fulfillment to people's lives. Adding ease. Adding wonder. Adding magic."

"I eventually want to be the anchor of the first trillion-dollar company."

"We all self-conscious. I'm just the first to admit it."

"Nothing in life is promised except death."

"I want to explain something about the title 'Yeezus', simply put 'West' was my slave name and 'Yeezus' is my God name."

"Pharrell has always been my style idol."

"Cause I want to be on 106 and Park pushing a Benz"

"If I do become more successful, either as a producer or a rapper, I'm going to do everything I can to help whoever I can on the label."

"It's so hard to do fittings for Yeezy because we want to do things that are inspiring, that people could look at and say, "Wow, I like that color palette, I could put that together." And there are so many images of things that it's almost impossible to have your clothes go up against the amount you're seeing and carry it into one language."

"The creative, they want to connect with people. These artists, the clothing designers, they want to connect with people the same way that music gets to connect with people. But the cost of silk is too expensive. And they won't lower their quality levels. So I can spend $2 million on a record and give it out in a democratic way. They could spend all their time making the greatest dress in the world, and it's just impossible to hand-make that many."

"Talking', talking, talking', talk. Baby, let's just knock it off. They don't know what we been through. They don't know 'bout me and you."

"I still think I am the greatest."

"If you ask me a question like what is your greatest accomplishment, it should be what I'm about to do"

"I would never want a book's autograph. I am a proud non-reader of books."

"My definition of genius is not being that person the actual human is a genius, but it's a person that just allows God to work through them."

"If everything I did failed - which it doesn't, it actually succeeds - just the fact that I'm willing to fail is an inspiration. People are so scared to lose that they don't even try. Like, one thing people can't say is that I'm not trying, and not I'm not trying my hardest, and I'm not trying to do the best way I know how."

"Everything in the world is exactly the same."

"The same people that tell me what I ought to have is the same people asking for an autograph."

"When I think of competition it's like I try to create against the past. I think about Michelangelo and Picasso, you know, the pyramids."

"I believe that bad taste is vulgar. It's like cursing. I think the world can be saved through design, because what is the most distasteful thing someone can do? Kill someone. So, good taste is the opposite of that."

"Fonts. I get emotional over fonts."

"If you know you're the best it only makes sense for you to surround yourself with the best. No Exceptions"

"Keep your nose out the sky, keep your heart to god, and keep your face to the raising sun."

"I don't know what's better getting' laid or getting' paid."

"My Caps Lock Key Is Loud!"

"I'm not going to be able to make things that I can call Kanye West just by making T-shirts."

"Maybe 90 percent of the time it looks like I'm not having a good time."

"Michael Jordan changed so much in basketball, he took his power to make a difference. It's so much going on in music right now and somebody has to make a difference."

"I'm the type of rock star that likes to have a girlfriend, you know?"

"It seem like everybody dress tight now, And I just want my credit."

"It's motivation. Some people are gifted at specific things, but I had to develop. The thing I'm most talented at is the ability to learn."

"I'm never at my worst because even at my lowest, its a learning experience. It's something that I'll bounce ideas off. I can take negatives and flip them to positives at all times."

"A lot of people are very sacred with their ideas, and there is something to protecting yourself in that way, but there's also something to idea sharing, or being the person who makes the mistake in public so people can study that."

"I hope we don't see no paparazzi today. Because I'm still getting acquainted with these jogging pants I threw on. Like, 'That's not my statement!'"

"I spent 80% of my time working on this, and 20% of my time working on music. Why do you think the song 'Niggas in Paris' is called 'Niggas in Paris?' 'Cause niggas was in Paris!"

"Clothing should be like food. There should never be a $5000 sweater. You know what should cost $5000? A car."

"If you have power, you have to empower."

"I'm supposed to be a musical genius, but I can't work the car seat that well."

"First rule in this world baby... don't believe anything you see on the news..."

"What I talked about in it was the idea of celebrity, and celebrities being treated like blacks were in the '60s, having no rights, and the fact that people can slander your name. I said that in the toast. And I had to say this in a position where I, from the art world, am marrying Kim. And how we're going to fight to raise the respect level for celebrities so that my daughter can live a more normal life. She didn't choose to be a celebrity. But she is. So I'm going to fight to make sure she has a better life."

"No flip flops for black dudes. I don't care where you at. Wear some hot ass Jordans on the beach."

"If you can focus the energy into something valuable, put that into work ethic ..."

"I am a pop artist, so my medium is public opinion and the world is my canvas"

"They classify my motivational speeches as rants!"

"The only luxury is time. The time you get to spend with your family."

"Having a Rolex or a Benz is not something that actually represents your success because there's always something more expensive to buy. Success is really being able to do things for others as well as the people around you and yourself."

"I want to tell the whole world about a friend of mine. This little light of mine, I'm feeling' let it shine. I'm feeling' take y'all back to them better times. I'm feeling' talk about my mama if y'all don't mind"

"There's a lack of creativity in every field because people are afraid. As an artist in this world we can do whatever we want"

"When we die, the money we can't keep, but we probably spend it all cause the pain aren't cheap."

"Like, I want the world to be better! All I want is positive! All I want is dopeness! Why would you want to control that?"

"Anytime I've had a big thing that's ever pierced and cut across the Internet, it was a fight for justice. Justice. And when you say justice, it doesn't have to be war. Justice could just be clearing a path for people to dream properly."

"I can sleep. I love sleep; it's my favorite."

"I'm the smartest celebrity you've ever dealt with. I'm not Britney Spears."

"I honestly feel that because Steve has passed, you know, it's like when Biggie passed and Jay-Z was allowed to become Jay-Z."

"I'm a monster, I'm a maven, I know this world is changing'. Never gave in, never gave up, I'm the only thing I'm afraid of."

"I'm living three dreams: Biggie Smalls', Dr. King, Rodney King's. Cause we can't get along, no resolution? Till we drown all these haters... Rest in peace to Whitney Houston"

"If you admire somebody, you should go ahead and tell them. People never get the flowers while they can still smell them."

"I believe in myself like a five-year-old believes in himself. They say look at me, look at me! Then they do a flip in the backyard. It won't even be that amazing, but everyone will be clapping for them."

"I feel like it's almost a Renaissance thing, a painting, a modern version of a painting. I think it's important for Kim Kardashian to have her figure. To not show it would be like Adele not singing."

"I think what Kanye West is going to mean is something similar to what Steve Jobs means. I am undoubtedly, you know, Steve of Internet, downtown, fashion, culture. Period. By a long jump. I honestly feel that because Steve has passed, you know, it's like when Biggie passed and Jay-Z was allowed to become Jay-Z."

"Even a broke clock is right twice a day"

"Rap is the new rock 'n' roll. We the real rock stars, and I'm the biggest of all of them. I'm the No. 1 rock star on the planet."

"I could let these dream killers kill my self-esteem, Or use my arrogance as the steam to power my dreams. I use it as my gas, so they say that I'm gassed, But without it I'd be last, so I ought to laugh..."

"Life is 5% what happens, and 95% how you react."

"I have this table in my new house. They put this table in without asking. It was some weird nouveau riche marble table, and I hated it. But it was literally so heavy that it took a crane to move it. We would try to set up different things around it, but it never really worked. I realized that table was my ego. No matter what you put around it, under it, no matter who photographed it, the douchebaggery would always come through."

"We're not always in the position that we want to be at. We're constantly growing We're constantly making mistakes. We're constantly trying to express ourselves and actualize our dreams."

"I hate when I'm on a flight and I wake up with a water bottle next to me like oh great now I got to be responsible for this water bottle"

"People always say that you can't please everybody. I think that's a cop-out. Why not attempt it? 'Cause think of all the people you will please if you try."

"We culture. Rap is the new rock 'n roll. We the rock stars. It's been like that for a minute, Hedi Slimane!"

"I'm a blowfish. I'm not a shark, I'm a blowfish."

"This is my life home, you decide yours"

"Criticism can bother you, but you should be more bothered if there's no criticism. That means you're too safe"

"I can be vilified. I can be misunderstood. I didn't come here to be liked. I came here to make a difference."

"If I were to write my title like going through the airport and you have to put down what you do? I would literally write 'creative genius' except for two reasons: Sometimes it takes too long to write that and sometimes I spell the word 'genius' wrong. The irony."

"God show me the way because the Devil trying to break me down"

"I make all my own decisions and I take full responsibility."

"I've got a million people telling me why I can't do it. You know, that I'm not a real designer, that I'm not this. I'm not a real rapper, either!"

"The longer your Gevity is, the more confidence you build."

"I think I started to approach time in a different way after the accident. Before I was more willing to give my time to people and things that I wasn't as interested in because somehow I allowed myself to be brainwashed into being forced to work with other people or on other projects that I had no interest in. So simply, the accident gave me the opportunity to do what I really wanted to do."

"I don't know if this is statistically right, but I'm assuming I have the most Grammys of anyone my age, but I haven't won one against a white person."

"It's only led me to complete awesomeness at all times. It's only led me to awesome truth and awesomeness. Beauty, truth, awesomeness. That's all it is."

"I'm doing pretty good as far as geniuses go ... I'm like a machine. I'm a robot. You cannot offend a robot ... I'm going down as a legend, whether or not you like me or not. I am the new Jim Morrison. I am the new Kurt Cobain ... The Bible had 20, 30, 40, 50 characters in it. You don't think that I would be one of the characters of today's modern Bible?"

"I'm the No. 1 artist in the world right now ... I am the No. 1 human being in music."

"I could never be in a situation with a job where I was not allowed to listen to music all day. I would rather work at a fast food restaurant where I could turn on the radio all day rather than be in a situation where I have to sneak and listen to music."

"The prettiest people do the ugliest things."

"I'm not a celebrity, I'm an activist. The fact that when I see truth it's really hard for me to sit back and just allow it to happen in front of me on my clock makes me, a lot of times, a bad celebrity."

"I'm a champion, so I turn tragedy to triumph."

"I wonder...would you rather have 100 from an average person or 10 from someone who is outstanding"

"I would like to thank Julius Caesar for originating my hairstyle"

"Sophisticated ignorance, write my curses in cursive."

"People don't stand up and protect their dreams because they get spoofed in a way."

"I can't be a slave to the machine, you feel like you're in the matrix."

"People in this world shun people for being great, for being a bright color, for standing out. But the time is now, to be OK with being the greatest you."

"I am God's vessel. But my greatest pain in life is that I will never be able to see myself perform live."

"Any woman that you're in love with or that loves you is going to command a certain amount of, you know, energy. It's actually easier to focus, in some ways."

"Success is the best revenge."

"Everyone's always telling you to be humble. When was the last time someone told you to be great?"

"I never seen snakes on a plane"

"Cause we they leaders, and they the followers And we the nut-busters and they the swallowers'"

"I don't care about having a legacy, I don't care about being remembered. The most important thing to me is, while we're here, while we're having fun, while we're sleeping, breathing oxygen, living life, falling in love, having pain and having joy...what can we do with our voice to make things easier, to help someone to make it better for our kids."

"The concept of commercialism in the fashion and art world is looked down upon. You know, just to think, 'What amount of creativity does it take to make something that masses of people like?' And, 'How does creativity apply across the board?'"

"We can teach about hip-hop history, we can teach about legends, hip-hop theory. It's been around so long that text books can be written about it. This is a perfect time to capitalize on and get kids excited about music education."

"I specifically ordered Persian rugs with cherub imagery!!! What do I have to do to get a simple Persian rug with cherub imagery ugh"

"You may be talented, but you're not Kanye West."

"I've been connected to the most culturally important albums of the past four years, the most influential artists of the past ten years. You have like, Steve Jobs, Walt Disney, Henry Ford, Howard Hughes, Nicolas Ghesquière, Anna Wintour, David Stern."

"If you can do it better than me, then you do it."

"If y'all fresh to death, then I'm deceased."

"To use is necessary. And if you can't be used, then you're useless."

"I think that's a responsibility that I have, to push possibilities, to show people: 'This is the level that things could be at.'"

"it wasn't until I hung out with Dead Prez and understood how to make, you know, raps with a message sound cool that I was able to just write "All Falls Down" in 15 minutes."

"I don't like to say something's weird when it's innovative and fresh."

"I completely lost everything, but I gained everything because I lost the fear."

"People will have a problem with whatever you do. At the end of the day, nobody can determine what you need to do in order to be successful and why would you listen to someone who is not successful tell you what you need to do?"

"Know your worth! People always act like they're doing more for you than you're doing for them."

"I knew when I wrote the line "light-skinned friend look like Michael Jackson" From the song "Slow Jamz" I was going to be a big star."

"Us as a people, we can't do it on our own. We have to understand that we're not each other's enemy. We have to stop discriminating against each other due to class and due to race and due to location or financial position."

"Went from most hated to the Champion God Flow, I guess that's a feeling' only me and LeBron know."

"'What you doing in the club on a Thursday?' She say she only here for her girl birthday... They ordered champagne but still look thirsty, Rock Forever 21 but just turned 30."

"I'm a pop enigma. I live and breathe every element in life. I rock a bespoke suit and I go to Harold's for fried chicken. It's all these things at once, because, as a taste maker, I find the best of everything."

"I am not what I would consider truly a musician. I am an inventor. I am an innovator."

"I'm a minimalist in a rapper's body."

""My Beautiful Dark Twisted Fantasy" and "Watch the Throne": neither was nominated for Album of the Year, and I made both of those in one year. I don't know if this is statistically right, but I'm assuming I have the most Grammys of anyone my age, but I haven't won one against a white person. But the thing is, I don't care about the Grammys; I just would like for the statistics to be more accurate."

"I'm talking' about us, the new slaves, the people who love fashion. I'm talking about us, you know? 'Cause I'm a slave to it. I love it."

"I am a God, so hurry up with my damn massage; in a French-ass restaurant, hurry up with my damn croissants."

"People say it takes a village to raise a child. People ask me how my daughter is doing. She's only doing good if your daughter's doing good. We're all one family."

"Taste and style is beyond clothes. It's in food; it's in quality. Working out, healthy bodies, organic food-they're all part of the same thing."

"I'm pretty calculating. I take stuff that I know appeals to people's bad sides and match it up with stuff that appeals to their good sides."

"I performed it all the way through for people. People would say, "We love you, we want to sign you," and then there'd always be one person who'd say, "He's just a producer.""

"What I had to learn from Kim is how to take more of her advice and less of other people's advice. There's a lot of Kim K skills that were added. In order to win at life, you need some Kim K skills, period."

"I live and breathe every element in life."

"I want to dress like a child as much as possible."

"Well, if someone has got all the money in the world, they'd still want love."

"That's very cool. Well, that's great. If I were to cater to Kanye, he would know that I'm catering to him. The fact that I make what I make-he gets it. He gets the quality and he respects it. And I think that's the key, why I work all the time is to do that. That's the fun."

"The hardest thing for me is to 'just' agree, and that is what sparks creativity, the feeling that something can be better, the feeling that something's missing, the feeling that something's needed."

"I thank Marc Jacobs so much for giving me the opportunity to design a shoe for Louis Vuitton, but the thing that broke my heart most was when they said, 'You're finished. The shoe's finished.'"

"Do you think there'd be a Givenchy in the hood if it wasn't for that South Park photo?"

"It's about whatever I want to make it about. It's my world."

"Shoot for the stars, so if you fall you land on a cloud."

EXTRAS

Author's Request

Our books are intended to indulge you. If you enjoyed this book or gained any valuable information from it in any way, feel free to share your experience with us. Your contented reviews will help to boost us not only in the sales perspective but also to improve our creativity. Please leave a review at the store front where you purchased this book and it would be greatly appreciated.

Related Books

Spellbinding Words of the Dragon: Bruce Lee Quotes for Everyone

by *Sreechinth C*

For common men, Bruce Lee is a martial arts icon and is renowned for his fearsome action in movies. Once we dip into the depth, it will be revealed that there persisted a philosopher inside Bruce. It was reflected in his talks, movies and the books he wrote. The 'Be Water my Friend', and 'a finger pointing at the moon' are some of the famous quotes he shared. This book is a compiled collection of his famous quotes of various genres like Motivational, Martial arts, Self Development, Spiritual, Love & Compassion, Learning & Hardworking, etc. With more than a hundred quotes, you will experience the philosophical wisdom of the perished Dragon who refuses to die from our thoughts.

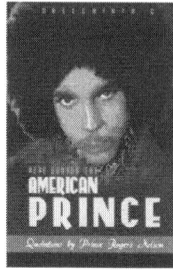

Here Quotes the American Prince: Quotations by Prince Rogers Nelson

by *Sreechinth C*

Seven time Grammy Award winner, Prince Rogers Nelson famous for his fusion music with controversial themes. Being internationally debuted with 'In For You' with Warner Bros, the later years seen him as the top in hits chart. He went off screen for some time and again hit back with his mesmerizing music. Converting his name to an unpronounceable love symbol, his triplets 'Emancipation', 'Crystal Ball' and 'Rave Un2 the Joy Fantastic' hit the buzz charts. Here in this book we have his fascinating words as his quotations...

When Words Dance – 500+ Madonna Quotes

by *Sreechinth C*

Madonna Ciccone, the Queen of Pop, came as a sensation in the male dominated music arena. With a the Guinness Record of world's best selling female recording artist, she is the wealthiest female musician of modern times. From a tough childhood, she rose to an international stardom just with reinventing and diversifying her talents. She excited her audience all over the world with numerous singles like "Like a Virgin", "Holiday" and "Material Girl". In this book 'When Words Dance – 500+ Madonna Quotes', we have the largest collection of the energetic words of this mesmerizing musician. Let's explore it...

Bob Marley Quotes: Abstract Lessons from Bob Marley

by *Sreechinth C*

It was in the eleventh day of the fifth month of 1981, malignant melanoma, a dangerous breed of cancer, took away the life of one of the most influential singer of the modern era, Robert Nesta "Bob" Marley. At that day, it was not just the 2 million Jamaicans who were shocked, the whole world wept with them, the whole world wept, hearing the early departure of the king of Reggae. Before he left us at the very age of 36, he contributed not only a collection of everlasting music, but also a cluster of memorable quotes which let us think, or feel the way he thought about the world and how he wanted us to inspire. Like we can feel Bob in his unique model songs, we can experience the mind state of Bob Marley in his sayings too. Though he perished, we can evocate his virtual self inside the realm of our mind.

76

The book, Bob Marley Quotes, is filled with his quotations on different categories like Music, Motivation, Religion, Inspiration, Humanity, Racism, Relationship, etc. This book will be a valuable collection for anyone who is fond of him or want to learn more about Bob

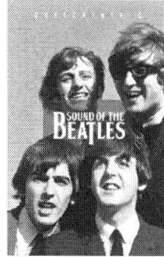

Sound of The Beatles: Quotes of John Lennon, Paul McCartney, Ringo Starr & George Harrison

by *Sreechinth C*

In the year of 1960 there boomed a new music band in the city of Liverpool which quickly blossomed and rocked the world of western music, The Beatles. Four youngsters, John Lennon, Paul McCartney, George Harrison and Ringo Starr created history when they teamed up together for the musical saga. They have received many awards which includes those of the pinnacle like Academy Award, and Grammy Awards. There are more achievements that they received, but the greatest was given by their fans, their love and affection which made The Beatles the biggest successful music band ever in western music. The vocal imprints Beatles left in the history and in the hearts of the music lovers is still intact even though the rock band was not lively intact for even a decade. After breakup of The Beatles, just like celestial objects, they persisted and moved on in the world of music as separate entities. Like their songs, their quotes were too meaningful. It is usual that people who met success think differently and the quotes of those who think different makes an average person open their thought process in divergent angles. This book, 'Sound of the Beatles: Quotes of John Lennon, Paul McCartney, Ringo Starr & George Harrison' contains the sayings and quotes of four of them, which is filled with thought generating sayings. Read through this book and discover what they have gifted us...

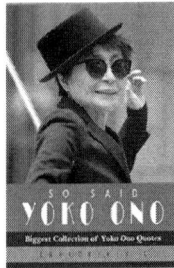

So Said Yoko Ono: Biggest Collection of Yoko Ono Quotes

by *Sreechinth C*

Yoko Ono, a Japanese singer, is well known to music world as the widow of John Lennon, the founder member of music band "The Beatles". The couple had gained attention through their protest to Vietnam War. Yoko is also commendable for her feministic ideas that she shared through her lyrics. Yoko Ono's charismatic personality reflects in her quotes also. Here we have collected sayings and quotes of Yoko Ono which consists of quotations about various topics like acting, movies, life, success, violence, god, relationship, and a lot more. You can find many motivational, humorous and mood shifting quotes among those she had spoken. This book, 'So Said Yoko Ono: Biggest Collection of Yoko Ono Quotes' contains the sayings and quotes of Yoko Ono, probably the biggest collection of Yoko Ono quotes that you can find.

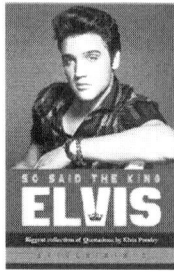

So said the King Elvis: Biggest collection of Quotations by Elvis Presley

by *Sreechinth C*

In the year of 1935, at Mississipi, there born Elvis Aaron Presley, who was virtually crowned as the King of Rock and Roll. Elvis Presley is counted as the most influential musician of the 20th century, better to say the most successful musical icon in the modern times. Elvis Presley still holds the record of best selling solo artist, with around six hundred million units sold across the globe. Not only music, he tried over film industry too. Elvis Presley holds three Grammy awards in his name along with many other achievements. The last days of Elvis were very tragic. The over usage of drugs had made a hell out of his life. When Elvis Presley left our world in the very age of 42, what he left for us was his music, memories, and his quotes. Here we have collected sayings and quotes of Elvis Presley which consists of quotations about various topics like music, life, social, truth, religion, success, relationship, money, etc. You can find some motivational and mood lifting quotes among those he had spoken. This book, 'So said the King Elvis: Biggest collection of Quotations by Elvis Presley' contains the sayings and quotes of Elvis Presley, probably the biggest collection of Elvis Presley quotes that you can find.. Spare some time for his wordings. Turn the pages and grasp the gifts that Elvis Presley had left for you...

Moss-less Quotes of the Rolling Stones

by *Sreechinth C*

The Rolling Stones is basically an English Band formed in the year 1962. Initially, Brian Jones, Ian Stewart, Mick Jagger, Keith Richards, Bill Wyman and Charlie Watts were the band members. The band gained popularity for their style and later for their music which were so youthful and defiant. Rolling Stones were able to make blue a part of rock and roll which brought revolution in the world of music. Later years, music lovers witnessed many of the best works of the Band in the late 1960's and early 1970's. Rolling Stones continued the path of making successful work till the Band parted during early 1980's. But by late 1980's they re united and regained their production of albums and stage performances. The Band gained much popularity by conducting live circuit performances in 1990's and 2000's. The Rolling Stones had received many honors and recognitions like, being enrolled into the Rock and Roll Hall of Fame in 1989 and UK Music Hall of Fame in 2004. This book 'Moss-less Quotes Of The Rolling Stones' is the greatest collection of quotes of the members of The Rolling Stone Band.

Best Works of the Publication

Spellbinding Words of the Dragon:
Bruce Lee Quotes for Everyone.

928 Maya Angelou Quotes (Ultimate Collection) (Volume 5)

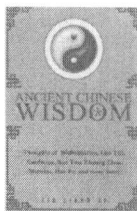

Ancient Chinese Wisdom:
Thoughts of Bodhidharma, Lao Tzu , Confucius, Sun Tzu, Zhuang Zhou, Mencius, Han Fei and many more

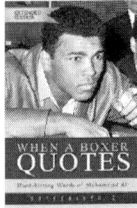

When a Boxer Quotes:
Hard-hitting Words of Muhammad Ali

Bob Marley Quotes:
Abstract Lessons from Bob Marley

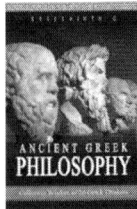

Ancient Greek Philosophy:
Collective Wisdom of 26 Greek Thinkers

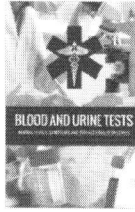

Blood And Urine Tests:
General Diagnostic Tests, Results and Diseases

Einstein Wisdom:
Quotes from an Extraordinary Brain

Dr Seuss Philosophy:
Witty Quotes by Dr Seuss

Sound of The Beatles:
Quotes of John Lennon, Paul McCartney, Ringo Starr & George Harrison

Enchanted Spells of an American Beauty:
Marilyn Monroe Quotes

The Vault of Walt Disney Quotes:
Best Walt Disney Quotes

Sadhguru Jaggi Vasudev Quotes

Ignited Quotes of Dr APJ Abdul Kalam

1395 Dalai Lama Quotes (Ultimate Collection) (Volume 1)

Printed in Great Britain
by Amazon

30132857R00058

Daisy Miller

Illustrated by **Marina Marcolin**

Retold by **Christopher Hall**
Activities by **Frederick Garland**

Editor: Tessa Vaughan
Design and art direction: Nadia Maestri
Computer graphics: Simona Corniola
Illustrations: Marina Marcolin
Picture research: Laura Lagomarsino

© 2006   Black Cat Publishing,
             an imprint of Cideb Editrice, Genoa, Canterbury

First edition : February 2006

Picture credits:
By courtesy of the National Portrait Gallery, London: 4;
© Francis G. Mayer/CORBIS: 49.

We would be happy to receive your comments and suggestions,
and give you any other information concerning our material.
editorial@blackcat-cideb.com
www.blackcat-cideb.com
www.cideb.it

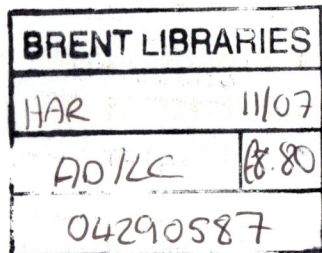

CISQ CISQCERT
TEXTBOOKS AND
TEACHING MATERIALS
The quality of the publisher's
design, production and sales processes has
been certified to the standard of
UNI EN ISO 9001

ISBN 88-530-0414-2   Book
ISBN 88-530-0413-4   Book + CD

Printed in Italy by Litoprint, Genoa